# BURNING SECRETS

### BY STEVE BREZENOFF

## ILLUSTRATED BY TOU VUE

**Librarian Reviewer**
Marci Peschke
Librarian, Dallas Independent School District
MA Education Reading Specialist, Stephen F. Austin State University
Learning Resources Endorsement, Texas Women's University

**Reading Consultant**
Elizabeth Stedem
Educator/Consultant, Colorado Springs, CO
MA in Elementary Education, University of Denver, CO

 **STONE ARCH BOOKS**
Minneapolis   San Diego

Vortex Books are published by Stone Arch Books,
A Capstone Imprint
151 Good Counsel Drive, P.O. Box 669
Mankato, Minnesota 56002
*www.capstonepub.com*

Copyright © 2008 by Stone Arch Books

All rights reserved. No part of this publication may be reproduced
in whole or in part, or stored in a retrieval system, or transmitted in any
form or by any means, electronic, mechanical, photocopying, recording,
or otherwise, without written permission of the publisher.

*Library of Congress Cataloging-in-Publication Data*
Brezenoff, Steven.
    Burning Secrets / by Steve Brezenoff; illustrated by Tou Vue.
    p. cm. — (Vortex Books)
    Summary: While cleaning up their great-great-uncle's house
in preparation for selling it, thirteen-year-old Roy and his eleven-
year-old brother, Jason, find two strange little doors and learn that
someone is trying to open them to get what lies between.
    ISBN-13: 978-1-59889-854-5 (library binding)
    ISBN-10: 1-59889-854-X (library binding)
    ISBN-13: 978-1-59889-920-7 (paperback)
    ISBN-10: 1-59889-920-1 (paperback)
    [1. Dwellings—Maintenance and repair—Fiction.
2. Supernatural—Fiction. 3. Ojibwa Indians—Fiction. 4. Indians
of North America—Great Lakes (North America)—Fiction.
5. Great Lakes Region (North America)—Fiction.] I. Vue,
Tou, 1974– ill. II. Title.
PZ7.M47833755 Bur 2008
[Fic]—dc22                                   2007006017

Art Director: Heather Kindseth
Graphic Designer: Kay Fraser

**Photo Credits**
Karon Dubke, cover (flames)
Kay Fraser, cover (book pages and trees)

Printed in the United States of America in Stevens Point, Wisconsin.
062011
006247R

# TABLE OF CONTENTS

# MANY YEARS AGO . . .

A full moon rose high above the Lakota village. In the shadow of a small tipi, a hut made of wooden poles and stretched animal skins, a young woman crouched. She listened to the excited voices coming from inside the tipi.

Her knees ached from sitting in that awkward position, but she had to wait for the voices to die down and the firelight to go out.

She held her infant son against her chest. For his very life, she had to wait.

< 5 >

Finally, after what seemed like hours, two men stomped angrily from the tipi. Soon after, the fire inside was extinguished.

The woman waited a few more minutes. She needed to be sure that the shaman, still inside the tipi, had gone to sleep. Then she bundled her son into the pack on her back and tiptoed around to the front of the hut.

As silently as she could, the young woman walked slowly into the tipi. She brushed aside the blanket hanging across the entrance and stepped inside. She heard the shaman's steady breathing as he slept.

Inside, the only light came from a few glowing embers in the dying fire.

The woman moved quietly to the middle of the tipi and pulled a log from beside the fire. She breathed a sigh of relief. The log was still intact. It had not completely burned away.

< 6 >

The young woman hugged the log against her chest, just as she had earlier hugged her infant son. He lay quietly on her back, unaware of his mother's strange behavior. Then the woman began to tiptoe out of the tipi.

Suddenly, the shaman was awake. He yelled, calling out an alarm. The woman's eyes opened wide, and she began to run.

The men of the village were all waking up. They ran out of their tipis. They yelled at her, ordering her to stop, but she didn't look back. She just held the log tightly against her chest and ran from the village into the dark, surrounding woods.

The men chased her, but she knew the woods well. She had played there many times as a small girl, and when she grew older, she had hunted those same woods to gather wood for the village fires.

< 7 >

Soon she came out on the far side of woods, where most of the villagers had never been. There was no one behind her.

For the moment, she was safe.

She turned and ran until the village was far behind her. Her infant son bounced on her back, laughing.

< 8 >

# CHAPTER 1

# THE GIANT HOUSE

Roy Blaze, thirteen years old, leaned on the hot window in the backseat of his mother's station wagon.

He and his eleven-year-old brother, Jason, had been in the car for hours, and the sun was beating down on them and the car's black leather seats.

"It's just around this bend, I think," said their mom. "I haven't been here since before you two were born!"

< 9 >

Roy rolled his eyes and Jason laughed.

"Boys," said their mom, "I know you'd rather spend your spring vacation at Water Park. Believe me, there are lots of things I'd rather do too. But you know I couldn't leave you two at home for a week."

"We know, Mom," the boys said.

"Okay," said their mom. "Then let's try to make this fun."

They had been planning for months to go to Water Park. Roy had been looking forward to riding the huge water slides, and Jason had been excited about the wave pool and the ice cream stand.

But when the boys' great-great-uncle passed away, leaving his house to them in his will, all their fun plans had been scrapped. They had to visit the house, clean it up, and get it ready to sell.

< 10 >

"I don't know why Uncle Mel left this house to us!" said Roy. "I never even met him."

"He never had any children of his own," said Mom. "As far as I know, we're his only living relatives."

Roy groaned.

He wasn't looking forward to a week of sweeping and scrubbing and painting inside a big smelly house, while all his friends were having fun miles away back home.

When the car turned the bend, the boys saw a gigantic old house, sitting atop a lonely hill.

Roy gasped.

Jason gulped. "Mom?" he said. "Is that the house?"

"Yup," she replied. "That's it."

"It's haunted!" said Jason.

< 11 >

"It is not!" said their mother, laughing.

"It sure looks like it is," said Jason.

Roy thought it looked haunted too, but he didn't want to seem scared.

The house was much bigger than their family house back in the city. Their uncle's house was four stories high with a big porch all around it. Only the top two stories had windows. At the top was a tall gray tower, with a window on each side and a black cone for a roof.

Mom pulled the car into the driveway and parked. "It sure does need some work," she said.

That's for sure, Roy thought.

"I hired a local painter to work on the outside," said Mom. "But you boys and I will have to do all the cleaning and painting on the inside."

< 12 >

< 13 >

Well, at least I won't have to climb all over the outside of the house, thought Roy. He was not a big fan of high places.

"Well, this should be an adventure," said Mom, starting up the front steps onto the porch. "Let's check out the inside!"

As she reached the third step, Roy heard a loud crack.

"Mom!" he called out. "Careful!"

Too late! There was another loud crack, and the steps collapsed.

Mom fell into the rubble.

< 14 >

# CHAPTER 2

# LARRY THE HANDYMAN

Jason screamed. Roy ran to the collapsed steps and called out, "Mom? Are you okay?"

"Yes," she said, and coughed. "I'm okay. Just a little banged up."

Roy lifted a few pieces of broken wood off his mom as she got to her feet and brushed herself off.

She limped over to the edge of the porch and sat down. Jason ran over and threw his arms around her.

< 15 >

Mom pulled her knee against her chest and hugged her leg. "Ow!"

"Do you think it's broken?" said Roy. "Your leg, I mean."

"I'm fine," said Mom. "It will probably just be a bad bruise. But maybe we should wait till tomorrow morning to start the cleaning."

Just then, a white pickup truck pulled into the driveway. On the side was painted "Larry the Handyman."

"Oh, that must be Larry Newcomb," said Mom as she stood up. "He's the painter I hired."

"Ms. Blaze?" said Larry as he climbed out of his truck.

He was very tall, over six feet, and very skinny. He had very dark hair, with specks of white paint in it, and it was very messy, as if he hadn't combed it in ages.

< 16 >

< 17 >

His white overalls were stained with paint blotches of many different colors. In his hand was a big wooden bucket, filled with brushes and some tools Roy didn't recognize.

"Hello, Mr. Newcomb," said Mom. "Thank you for coming." She pointed at the porch steps. "We had a little problem with the front steps. They just collapsed."

Larry let out a low whistle. "That's a shame," he said. "I hope you weren't hurt."

But, Roy noticed, Larry smiled slightly when he said it.

"Just bruised, I think," said Mom. "Do you think this is something you can fix?"

Larry looked at the broken steps. Then he looked at the boys.

"I think I can fix it," he said, still smiling. "Of course, I'd have to charge you for the lumber I'll have to buy."

< 18 >

Mom sighed. "Well, I guess that's the way it will have to be," she said. "We can't sell a house without front steps."

Larry put down his bucket and went back to his truck. Roy watched him take the ladder out of the truck.

"I think I'll find my bedroom and lie down for a while," said Mom. "You boys bring in the bags and find your room. You can explore the house all you want, just make sure to stay out of Mr. Newcomb's way."

After bringing in their bags and Mom's bag, Roy and Jason started checking out all the rooms in the house. "Let's start in the basement," said Roy. "Then we can work our way up and finish in the attic."

"The basement?" said Jason. "I don't know. Let's start someplace safe, like the kitchen. Or the TV room."

< 19 >

"There is no TV room, Jay," said Roy. "Uncle Mel was like a hundred years old. He never got a TV."

"But the basement?" said Jason, trembling. "That's the creepiest place in the house! That's where all the ghosts probably hang out during the day."

"There are no ghosts, Jay!" Roy started down the front hall toward the basement steps. "Sheesh, grow up, will you?"

Roy opened the door to the basement and headed down the stairs.

Suddenly Jason was all alone in the front hall. The dusty light over his head wasn't working, and creepy shadows crawled over him.

When he saw a big black spider dangling from the ceiling, he cried out. "Wait! Don't leave me here!"

< 20 >

# CHAPTER 3

# THE GOBLIN'S DOOR

The basement was just a cluttered, dusty room full of very old books.

Roy looked through some of them, but nothing caught his interest. Jason barely moved from his older brother's side, though Roy didn't see anything to be afraid of.

Roy put down an ancient issue of the *Saturday Evening Post*. "Well, this is boring. Let's go up and check out the first floor," he said.

< 21 >

"Finally!" said Jason. In seconds he was up the steps and out of the basement.

Roy caught up and together they went into the kitchen.

Roy opened the fridge. "Empty!"

Jason opened a big door on the other side of the room. "The pantry is empty too."

Roy came up beside him. "Well, at least we won't have to clean out a bunch of old nasty food."

Jason said, "Yup." He pushed open a swinging door, revealing the dining room.

Heavy, dusty curtains covered the windows, so no sunlight could reach into the room at all.

There were stacks of old books, like the ones in the basement, piled on the big oak table in the middle of the room.

< 22 >

A cabinet against the wall held dozens of statues.

"Cool!" said Jason. He ran to the cabinet and ran his fingers over the stone statues.

Roy walked over to the statues to take a closer look.

Jason grabbed one of the statues off the cabinet and wiped off some dust. "Wow, this baby's heavy!" he said.

Roy picked up another one. It was a stone statue of a man's head, wearing an animal skin. Roy thought it was about two feet tall.

"What have you boys found?" Larry Newcomb had come into the dining room from the kitchen. He was holding a cup of water.

"Just some crummy old statues," said Roy.

Larry let out a whistle.

< 23 >

"They don't look crummy to me," he said.

He picked one up and looked it over closely. It was a young boy about Roy's age, and he was carrying a deer around his neck, as if he'd just come from hunting.

"Looks like Indian, probably Lakota," said Larry, placing it back on the cabinet where he'd found it. "I bet they're worth a fortune."

Larry gulped back his water, crushed the cup in his hand, and nodded at the boys. Then he swung open the kitchen door and left.

Roy watched the door swing shut, then looked closely at the statue Larry had held.

"I wonder if they really are worth anything," he said.

"Mom will know," said Jason. "Hey, look at this!" Jason moved aside a couple of statues that stood on the floor next to the cabinet.

< 24 >

Behind the statues stood a little wooden door, about two feet high.

"What do you think that's for?" asked Jason.

"Santa's elves?" said Roy, with a laugh.

"More like creepy little elves in a place like this," said Jason. "More like goblins, or gremlins, or trolls, or . . ."

"Okay, okay, I get the picture," said Roy.

Both boys cleared away a few more statues, moving them to the table.

They had trouble balancing them on all the old books, but they seemed okay.

"Let's open it," said Roy.

Jason grabbed the tiny doorknob in the middle of the door and tugged.

The door wouldn't budge.

< 25 >

"It's locked," Jason said.

"Let me try," said Roy. He pushed his little brother out of the way.

Jason fell back and hit his head on the table. "Ow!" he yelled. One of the statues teetered and fell onto the floor, making a loud thump.

"What's going on?" yelled their mom. They heard her coming down the main stairs.

"Roy pushed me into the table!" Jason yelled. He walked out of the dining room and into the front hall to meet their mom. She was still limping from her fall on the front steps.

"I didn't push him," said Roy, following him. "It was an accident!"

"I don't want to hear about it," said Mom. She sighed. "We have a lot of work to do, and only five days to do it. I need you boys to stay out of trouble!"

< 27 >

Mom went on, "Roy, we need to find some old brooms. I'm not using my good brooms on these filthy floors. See if you can find anything in that closet." She pointed to a door under the front hall stairs.

"Okay," replied Roy.

The closet door stuck a little, but when Roy pulled harder, it suddenly came open. A cloud of dust billowed out and made him cough.

The closet was huge. It took up all the space under the steps, from the ceiling right down to where the lowest step met the floor. There were spiderwebs everywhere.

"Ugh," said Roy.

He stepped into the closet and spotted some brooms in the far corner. The two brooms looked like they'd been made a thousand years ago. A dustpan was there too, but it was all cracked and broken. It looked useless.

< 28 >

"We should have brought a vacuum cleaner," he said to himself.

Roy grabbed both brooms and the dustpan.

As he was turning to leave, he noticed a little door on the far wall, below the highest part of the steps.

The door looked just like the one Jason had found in the dining room.

Roy propped the brooms against the wall and walked up to the little door. He grabbed the doorknob.

The knob was vibrating.

Weird, thought Roy.

It reminded him of how the refrigerator back home felt when he put his hand against its side. A constant, low vibration. Roy pressed his ear against the door and heard a swooshing sound, like a motor running.

< 29 >

He jiggled the doorknob.

This door was locked too.

"Roy!" called Mom. "Did you find anything?"

Roy pulled on the little door one more time, but it didn't budge.

"Coming, Mom!" He grabbed the brooms and dustpan and hurried out into the living room where Mom and Jason were waiting for him. The three of them started cleaning.

Mom smiled and said, "And once we've finished here, we only have twenty more rooms to go."

< 30 >

## CHAPTER 4

# THE OLD MAN

That night, the three Blazes ate dinner at Roscoe's, a diner down on Main Street in town.

Jason said the place looked like it was a hundred years old, but it was bright and clean. They sat in a booth with high back seats covered in crackly, red leather.

Roy thought the fried chicken was dry, but from the way Jason was eating, the macaroni and cheese was the best in the world.

Mom hardly touched her food.

< 31 >

She seemed like she was in a bad mood, pushing her mashed potatoes around with her fork and running her fingers through her hair.

"What's the matter, Mom?" asked Roy.

"What?" said Mom. "Oh, nothing. Nothing's wrong." She straightened her napkin on her lap. "I guess I didn't realize how tough it would be to get Uncle Mel's house cleaned up to sell," she said.

Mom smiled, but Roy thought she wasn't telling him what was really bothering her.

When Mom got up to use the bathroom, Roy turned to Jason, who was sitting next to him in the booth. "What do you think is wrong with Mom?" Roy asked.

Jason shrugged. "I don't know. Maybe her leg is bugging her." Jason was shoveling macaroni and cheese into his mouth as fast he could.

< 32 >

Roy scrunched up his face. He noticed Mom wasn't limping when she walked to the bathroom.

"No," he said. "Her leg seems almost all better. I bet that weirdo Larry is charging her a lot to fix the porch."

"Could be," said Jason through his food.

"Maybe Mom could make some extra money selling those statues," Roy said.

"Cool idea," said Jason.

Just then, someone tapped Roy on the shoulder. He turned to look, and staring back at him was the oldest, most wrinkled man he'd ever seen.

"Roy Blaze," the old man said. His voice sounded old and dry, like dust in a forgotten closet. Like he hadn't spoken in a century.

Jason kept shoveling food in his mouth.

< 33 >

"How do you know my name?" said Roy.

The old man slowly smiled, and his lips and cheeks cracked. "I just thought I'd welcome you to town," he said. "Nice to have a new family moving here."

He leaned very close to Roy when he spoke. His breath smelled like an attic, and it was very cold.

"Oh, we're not moving here," said Roy. "We're just fixing up my uncle Mel's house and then selling it. He died."

The old man leaned even closer. "Oh," he said. "Did he?" Roy felt the man's cold breath on his neck and shivered. The boy nodded in reply.

"What a pity," said the old man. "I knew Mel Blaze very well . . . once."

Roy squinted at the old man. "Once?"

< 34 >

The man nodded slowly and smiled, showing his few, stained teeth.

"Gross!" whispered Jason in his brother's ear.

Roy elbowed him in the stomach and whispered back, "Quiet!"

"Mel was very stubborn," the old man went on. "I loved him very much at one time, and I know he loved me. But, well, things change."

"What's that crazy guy talking about?" whispered Jason.

"Eat your macaroni and cheese," said Roy.

Roy turned to the old man who was still standing close by their booth.

He seemed so old and frail, that Roy thought if someone bumped into him the old man might crumble away.

< 36 >

He reminded Roy of the stiff, dusty statues that crowded Uncle Mel's old dining room.

"So, what happened?" Roy asked. "What changed between you and Uncle Mel?"

The old man shrugged and smiled. "That's family for you," he said.

Then he lifted a wrinkled, sharp finger and pointed toward the back of the diner. "Here comes your mother. I'd better go," he said.

Roy looked up to see his mom heading back to the table, but by the time he turned back to the old man, the stranger had vanished.

< 37 >

# CHAPTER 5

# A STRANGER INSIDE

That night, Roy lay awake in his bed. He could hear Jason breathing in his bed across the room they shared. But Roy couldn't sleep.

He kept thinking about the old man from the diner.

Why did he just run off? Was he afraid of Mom seeing him? And what did he have to do with Uncle Mel?

If he was in Uncle Mel's family, didn't that mean he was in Roy's family, too?

Roy wondered how large the Blaze family was. Could there be cousins and uncles and aunts he didn't even know? But Mom had said they were Uncle Mel's only relatives.

Why didn't Uncle Mel leave the house to the old man? He lived right in town!

Suddenly, Roy's thoughts were interrupted by a soft thump from the backyard. It sounded like someone was walking behind the house.

Roy and Jason were staying in an old bedroom that faced the backyard.

They were on the third floor, so they had a window that overlooked the dark trees surrounding the house.

Roy pushed off his blankets and headed to the window. Pushing aside the curtain, he saw the backyard lit by half a moon.

A shadowy figure moved in the woods behind the house.

< 39 >

The figure seemed to be carrying something, like a toolbox, and he was heading toward the back door.

Roy went over and gave his brother a shake. "Jay," he whispered. "Jay, wake up."

Jason opened his eyes and yawned. "Roy?" He stretched his arms. "What's the matter?"

Roy covered his brother's mouth. "Shh. Someone's in the backyard. I think he's going to try to break in!"

"We have to wake up Mom!" said Jason.

"No way," replied Roy. Jason could be such a baby sometimes. "We can handle it."

Besides, thought Roy, Mom's been in such a bad mood. She wouldn't like to be woken up in the middle of the night.

The brothers crept out of the room and down the stairs.

< 40 >

As they reached the bottom, Roy peeked around the corner and saw a figure through the window in the back door. The figure was hunched over, and Roy heard some scraping at the doorknob.

It jiggled.

Roy knew the man was going to try to pick the lock.

"He really is trying to break in," Roy whispered. "I have an idea. Come on."

The boys tiptoed through the living room into the dining room.

"Now, do what I do," Roy said to his little brother.

Roy grabbed one of the statues and waited by the door that led to the kitchen.

He had a feeling that the man at the back door would come into the dining room.

< 41 >

After all, that's where all the expensive statues were being kept. Roy held the statue over his head, ready to fight.

Jason watched his older brother. Then he picked up a statue too. He held it up, ready to drop it on the burglar's foot.

Suddenly the boys heard a click.

"He's in the house," whispered Roy. "He just turned the light on in the kitchen. Get ready!"

The door from the kitchen started to swing open. Light flooded the dining room.

"Now!" yelled Roy.

He swung the statue as the door opened farther and the mystery person walked into the dining room.

"Aaah!"

Roy stopped his swing in midair.

< 42 >

< 43 >

"Roy Blaze, what in the world are you doing?"

"Mom!" shouted Roy in surprise. "What are you doing here?"

"What am I doing here?" she yelled. "I came down for some water and I heard you boys sneaking around in the dining room!"

"Oh," said Roy. "We were just, um . . ."

Mom didn't let Roy finish. "Why did you just attack me with a statue?" She was furious.

Roy put the statue back on the table. "I saw someone trying to break in the back door!"

Jason put down his statue and looked down at the floor.

Mom looked down at Roy. Her eyes were narrow and her eyebrows were up. Roy knew she didn't believe him.

< 44 >

"It's the truth, Mom," said Roy. "You must have scared him off when you turned on the kitchen light!"

"Not another word," snapped Mom. "Get back upstairs right now."

\* \* \*

Roy's heart was racing, and he was sure he'd never fall asleep.

He did, though, and he dreamed about the old man from the diner.

The man was sitting at a big campfire, and the light was dancing on his old, worn face.

When the old man noticed Roy, he looked up at him and laughed. It sounded friendly, and it reminded Roy of his grandfather.

Suddenly, the old man pointed at something behind Roy.

Roy turned.

< 45 >

He saw a creeping figure in the woods. Its back was hunched over, and it was holding something in its arms.

He couldn't tell if it was a man or a woman.

"Get a closer look, Roy Blaze," said the old man from behind him. Then he laughed again.

Roy started walking toward the woods.

The figure seemed to be running away from him.

"Wait!" Roy called, but the figure didn't listen. It just kept running, deeper into the woods.

* * *

A huge crash woke Roy just before dawn.

Roy and Jason tore into the hallway. Their mom was already there.

< 46 >

"Did you boys hear that crash?" she whispered.

The brothers nodded. Jason looked very scared.

"Okay," said Mom. "You boys wait in my bedroom while I call the police."

After a few minutes they heard a knock on the front door.

< 47 >

# CHAPTER 6

# SHERIFF NEWCOMB

"Mrs. Blaze?" said the policeman at the door. He was very fat.

Roy couldn't imagine this fat man chasing down a crook if his life depended on it.

"I'm Sheriff Bob Newcomb," said the fat policeman.

He took off his hat and revealed a big bald head, with a few shaggy strands of hair that stuck out around the edges.

"Hello, Sheriff," replied Mom.

Mom paused, thinking. Then she said, "Newcomb. Are you related to Larry Newcomb, the handyman?"

The sheriff stammered for a moment. "Oh," he said, "um, yes. He's my brother."

Roy eyed the sheriff suspiciously.

"So, tell me what's going on here," Sheriff Newcomb said.

Mom explained the loud crash they'd heard and said she thought it had come from the dining room.

"Then Jason and I heard a prowler last night," said Roy.

His mom shushed him. "Quiet, Roy," she said. "Let the sheriff do his job."

The four of them went into the dining room. The sheriff drew his nightstick, ready to defend them.

< 49 >

He held his finger to his lips, motioning them to be quiet. Then he swung the door open and shouted, "Freeze!"

The room was empty.

"He escaped!" said Roy.

The sheriff nodded. Then he stooped over with a grunt and picked up a statue off the ground. "If someone was here at all," he said.

"What do you mean?" said Mom. "We heard a prowler!"

The sheriff frowned. "Or you heard these statues falling off the table," he said.

Roy squinted at the sheriff. He didn't trust him.

"See how shaky they are, sitting here?" the sheriff said. To demonstrate, he tapped one of the statues on the table with his pinky. It fell off the table with a big crash.

< 50 >

Jason looked up at Roy and shook his head.

"But, Sheriff," said Roy, "we saw the man prowling around last night."

"You did, did you?" said the sheriff. "Well then, tell me, son. If there was a burglar here, why did he leave all these statues? Old Man Blaze's statue collection is famous around here. It's worth a fortune."

A fortune? thought Roy. Wow!

"Are any of the statues missing?" asked the sheriff.

Roy looked at the collection. "I don't know," he said. "We've only been here one day. We don't know the collection very well!"

In truth, Roy didn't know if any statues were missing. If the crook had taken only one or two, he never would have noticed.

< 52 >

"We never counted them," said Jason.

"Hmm," said Mom to Sheriff Newcomb. "I guess you might be right. It could have just been these statues falling onto the floor."

"Mom!" said Roy.

"That's enough, Roy," said Mom. Then she turned to the sheriff. "Thank you, Sheriff Newcomb. We're sorry to have gotten you up so early."

The sheriff walked to the door and tipped his big hat at the three of them. "All part of the job."

After the sheriff had left, Mom said, "Well, I don't think I'll get back to sleep, and it's morning anyway. I suppose we might as well have breakfast. Let's all get dressed, and then we'll go to the diner in town."

When their mom was climbing the stairs, the boys scurried into the dining room.

< 53 >

Jason called his brother over to the cabinet. "Look at this, Roy."

Roy joined his brother and saw scratches around the tiny door behind the statues.

"Someone tried to break in there," said Jason. He tugged the knob, but the door still wouldn't budge.

"Looks like he didn't succeed," Roy said.

< 54 >

## CHAPTER 7

# SHOCK

During breakfast at the diner, Larry Newcomb came in and ordered a cup of coffee at the counter.

Roy could see right into his tool bucket, which sat beside him on the floor.

He elbowed his brother.

"Ow!"

"Look at that," said Roy, pointing at the bucket.

"What?" said Jason.

< 55 >

He looked around, then sounding surprised, asked, "Mr. Newcomb's tools?"

"Right. See that funny metal one sticking up?" said Roy.

Jason nodded. Roy went on, "Doesn't it look like it could have made those scratches on the little door in the dining room?"

"I guess," Jason said.

"And remember how excited Larry got about the statues?" Roy continued. "He probably plans to steal them and sell them. He thinks he can get rich."

Jason pushed his spoon through his cereal. "That crook," he muttered.

Roy nodded. "And I'll bet Sheriff Newcomb is protecting his brother."

Jason nodded and spooned some cereal into his mouth.

< 56 >

"But what would he want behind that door?" mumbled Roy. "The statues were all out in plain sight."

"Maybe there's a treasure back there," Jason said with a full mouth. "The best statue of all. Or maybe it leads to a secret room full of statues. And maybe those statues are all made of gold and . . ."

"Hello, Roy." Suddenly the old man was back, and he was standing next to their booth. "Having breakfast?"

The old man's voice gave Roy the chills.

He looked even older today. His eyes were sunken and very dark. His skin was pale, the colors of ashes. His head and skin were all dry and cracked.

It made him look like a living, breathing skeleton.

"Yes, we are," replied Roy.

< 57 >

"Where's your mother this morning?" said the old man.

Roy looked up, and sure enough, his mother wasn't at the table anymore.

Surprised, he glanced around the diner and finally spotted her at the far end of the counter. She was probably ordering some sandwiches for their lunch later that day.

"She's over there," said Roy.

The old man smiled, and Roy thought he could hear his skin cracking.

"I heard you folks had a prowler last night," said the old man. "Did the sheriff find any clues?"

"No," said Roy. "He thinks no one broke in at all."

"Oh really?" said the old man. "But you don't agree?"

< 58 >

Roy shook his head. "No, I don't." He glanced at Larry at the counter.

The old man turned to look at Larry. His bones creaked and popped. "The sheriff's brother," he said. "I remember when those two were boys, about your ages."

He squinted at Jason and smiled.

Roy looked over at his mother and wished she'd hurry up.

"The two of them got into quite a bit of trouble together back then," the old man continued. "We all called them the 'Newcomb Twosome'!"

He leaned close to Roy's face, and his cold breath made Roy shiver.

"We were all surprised when Bobby ran for sheriff," he said. "We were even more surprised when he won."

< 59 >

The old man put his bony hand on Roy's shoulder. "What does our good sheriff think happened at your house last night?"

Roy could hardly get his mouth to work, but he finally said in a whisper, "He thinks we were only hearing the old statues falling off the table."

"Ah, yes, those old statues. Mel loved his statues. Sometimes he loved them better than people."

The old man stood up straighter. Even when he was standing up as straight as he could, he was very bent over.

"You boys should probably let Bobby handle things like this from now on," the old man said.

"Okay," said Roy, but he didn't really plan to stay out of it.

"That's the boy," said the old man.

< 60 >

He smiled creepily at Roy. "Stay out of trouble." And he walked off.

Roy watched him walk over to a light fixture near the kitchen.

The old man had trouble walking, and seemed to be dragging one leg.

"I got us some ham sandwiches for lunch," said Mom as she sat down. "Are you boys done with your breakfast yet?"

Jason nodded. He'd eaten his cold cereal in record time.

"I'm just about done," said Roy, shoveling scrambled eggs into his mouth. "Mom, do you know who that old man is? The one over there?" he added.

Mom turned. "He works here in the diner, I guess," she said. "Looks like he's fixing the light."

< 61 >

Roy watched the man as he climbed a ladder and jammed a screwdriver right into a light socket.

Roy saw sparks flying. Suddenly Roy could see through the man, as if he had x-ray vision.

He could see the old man's bones!

For a moment, every inch of the old man was lit up like a Halloween skeleton that glowed in the dark.

A moment later, everything was normal again.

No one else in the diner seemed to have noticed.

Then the old man pulled a bulb from the pocket of his denim overalls and screwed it into the fixture. The light shined on the old man's face, making deep shadows under his eyes and mouth.

< 62 >

The old man looked over at Roy and smiled.

Roy shuddered.

"He must be over a hundred years old," he said to his mom.

But his mom was already on her feet. "Are you coming, Roy?" she called to him as she reached for the door.

He didn't even get a shock, thought Roy. That old man looked like he'd been struck by lightning!

And that live light fixture should have knocked him right off the ladder.

It should have killed him!

< 64 >

# CHAPTER 8

# THE SCRAPER

After sweeping the kitchen, the den, and the study, the Blazes decided to stop for lunch and have their sandwiches from the diner.

Roy went to put the brooms back under the stairs. When he got there, he stared at the little door.

He propped the brooms in the corner and grabbed the little doorknob. It wouldn't budge.

If I could only see a little bit of what's behind there, he said to himself.

< 65 >

Roy looked up over his head and spotted a string hanging from the highest part of the ceiling.

He jumped a couple of times, but he found he couldn't reach it.

"Darn," he said.

He tried the doorknob one more time, pulling so hard that he slipped and fell.

But the door still didn't budge.

He would come back with Jason to help him reach the light.

* * *

The ham sandwiches were about as dry as the fried chicken had been.

But the lunch break was nice.

Roy, Jason, and their mom set up an old bedsheet on the back lawn and made a little picnic.

< 66 >

Even Larry Newcomb, who spotted the family from his perch high on a ladder, came and joined them.

He had a thermos of iced tea with him, and he gave each of them a big cup.

"My brother told me about what happened here the other night," Larry said. "About the break-in."

Mom nodded. "Yes," she said. "Boy, did I feel foolish."

Roy rolled his eyes and Jason laughed.

Roy glanced at Larry's tool bucket. "Say, Mr. Newcomb," he said. "What is that tool there? The metal one sticking up."

Larry looked down into his bucket.

"This one?" he said, pulling out a tool with a wide flat head and long handle.

Roy nodded.

< 67 >

"It's a paint scraper," said Larry. "I use this to remove the old dry paint before I put the new paint on the house."

"Can I see it?" asked Roy.

Larry glanced at the boys' mom. Then he shrugged. "I guess so," he said, and handed it over to Roy.

Roy examined it closely, and Jason leaned over to get a look too.

The sharp end of the scraper was very scratched up. "How did this happen?" asked Roy. He pointed to the chipped end.

"Just the way it goes," said Larry. "Sometimes I have to get a little rough with my tools to get the work done."

He got to his feet. "Well, I guess I've taken a long enough break. Better get back to work!" He reached for his scraper.

< 68 >

Roy took another quick look at the tool before he handed it over.

Larry said, "If you ever want a lesson in house painting, and if it's okay with your mom, I'd be happy to show you a few things."

Then he turned and headed back to his ladder.

* * *

Later that afternoon, Roy was in the backyard rinsing out some mops when Larry came down from painting the outside of the house.

"Mr. Newcomb?" said Roy, dropping the mop he was cleaning onto the lawn.

Larry looked up as he was sorting through his tools and paintbrushes. "Yeah?"

"I found the weirdest thing this morning, in the dining room," Roy said.

< 69 >

"What's that?" said Larry, cleaning off his paintbrushes in a bucket of smelly liquid.

"Scratch marks on the wall, next to a tiny door," Roy said.

He watched Larry's face closely for a reaction.

"This is an old house," Larry said. "I'm sure it's been scratched and knocked and banged up a lot."

"It's just the scratches," said Roy. "I thought they looked like they could have been made by that scraper of yours."

Suddenly Larry twisted around and leaned into Roy's face.

"What are you trying to say?" the man asked angrily.

"Um, nothing," Roy stammered.

< 71 >

"That's why you were looking at my scraper earlier," said Larry.

"No, that's not true!" Roy replied.

"Just stay out of my way, kid," said Larry. "You got that?"

Roy didn't say anything. He just gulped hard, and Larry headed back to his ladder.

< 72 >

# CHAPTER 9

# SCRATCHES

The next morning, Mom woke up the boys for breakfast.

"I've been out already this morning," she said as they all went downstairs. "I ran to the store on Main Street to get some groceries so we wouldn't have to keep eating that awful diner food!"

"You left us alone all morning?" said Jason. "You never leave us alone at home!"

"You weren't alone," Mom said.

< 73 >

Mom pulled some eggs and bacon out of the fridge. "Mr. Newcomb was here the whole time, working on the front steps," she said. "You were perfectly safe."

Right, thought Roy, perfectly safe with the burglar.

Jason looked at him with big worried eyes.

* * *

After breakfast, Roy went out to the yard to get the mops he'd rinsed the day before.

As he was picking them up, he overheard Larry talking on his cell phone from the side yard of the house.

"That older kid is driving me crazy, Bobby," he was saying.

He must be talking to his brother, the sheriff, thought Roy.

There was a long pause.

< 74 >

Roy assumed the person on the other end was talking. Then Larry spoke again: "I have to get this job done today, or it's all over."

Another pause.

"I'll get to work on it right now! Okay, Bobby. Don't worry. I'll make sure it gets done," Larry said.

Roy heard Larry snap his phone shut and start walking toward the backyard.

Roy quickly gathered up the mops and ran into the house.

Mom was cleaning up the breakfast dishes, so Roy told Jason everything he'd heard on the phone.

"What do you think it means?" asked Jason. The noise from the running water and the clanking dishes drowned out the boys' talking, so Mom couldn't hear them.

< 75 >

"Don't you get it?" Roy said. "Larry is worried I'm onto him, because of what I said yesterday. Now he has to hurry to get the job done today!"

"The job?" said Jason.

Roy rolled his eyes. "That's how crooks talk about their plans to rob a place," he explained. "They call it a 'job'.'"

Suddenly the sink shut off. "Jason, go and get the cleaning supplies from the closet," Mom said.

Jason left the kitchen, and after a couple of minutes, Roy heard him cry out.

"Roy! Come quick!"

Roy ran into the closet. It was even more of a mess than usual. The brooms had been knocked over, a shelf along the back hall had been broken, and loads of small tools were scattered all over the floor.

< 76 >

"Look at this!" shouted Jason. He pointed to the little door.

"I already know about the little door," said Roy.

"No, I mean look at this," said Jason. Roy moved closer.

Next to the doorknob and all along the edges of the door were scratches.

"Do you think whoever broke in the other night did this too?" asked Jason.

Roy shook his head. "How could they?" he said. "I would have noticed. I'm in here twice a day to get the cleaning supplies and put them away again. This closet wasn't like this yesterday."

Roy thought for a moment. "It must have been Larry. He was the only one here this morning besides us!"

< 77 >

Jason shook his head. "I don't know. We would have heard him! Look at the mess he made."

"I know!" said Roy. "It must have happened while you and I were asleep. Remember? Mom was at the grocery store and left us here alone with him."

Jason looked at the little door.

"Where do you suppose these doors go?" he said.

"I don't know," said Roy.

"They must go to the same place," said Jason. "They're on the same wall."

Roy thought for a moment.

"Hey," he said, "you're right."

I guess Jason isn't so dumb after all, he thought.

"Maybe it's the same door," said Jason.

< 79 >

He paused, thinking. Then he said, "Maybe this one just opens to the dining room, and that other one just opens to this closet."

"Hmm," said Roy. "I have an idea."

He darted out of the closet to the dining room, and then rushed right back.

"The wall is really thick between them. There must a small secret compartment in that wall," Roy said.

Jason nodded and smiled.

Roy stuck his hands in his pockets. "Larry must want whatever's in there. Tonight we're going to find out what that is."

< 80 >

## CHAPTER 10

# THE FOUNTAIN

That night Roy lay awake, watching the light from his mom's room shining into the hall.

As soon as he heard the click and saw the light turn off, he threw off his blanket and tiptoed over to his brother's bed.

"Jason," he whispered, tapping his brother's shoulder. "Wake up."

"What time is it?" asked Jason, blinking his eyes.

< 81 >

"After midnight, I think," replied Roy. "Mom just went to sleep. Time for me and you to get to work."

Jason yawned and got to his feet. "Okay," he mumbled. "Let's go."

Roy and Jason crept downstairs, and then quietly opened the closet under the stairs. The door squeaked horribly. For a moment Roy was sure Mom would wake up. The boys stood totally still for what seemed like ages, but when Mom didn't come downstairs, they stepped into the closet.

"Leave the door open, so we have some light," said Roy.

"Don't worry about that," replied Jason. "I don't want to get locked in this creepy closet!"

Roy pulled an old screwdriver out of his pants pocket. He had snuck the tool into his bedroom earlier that day.

< 82 >

Quickly he went to work on the door, first hacking at the doorknob, then working on the hinges.

After what seemed like an hour of sweaty work, one hinge popped off.

"You got it!" shouted Jason.

"Shhh!" Ray hissed. "You'll wake Mom up."

The boys stood still again, listening, to make sure their mom hadn't woken up.

After a few minutes of silence, Roy started working again. He jammed the screwdriver between the door and wall and pulled, using the screwdriver like a lever.

Finally the door sprung open with a sigh. Beyond the door it was pitch dark.

The boys could hear a small motor working, and what sounded like running water. But they couldn't see anything.

< 83 >

"Here," said Roy. "Climb up on my shoulders and turn on the light."

Roy gave his brother a boost and soon the closet light was on.

"Weird," said Roy.

"What is it?" asked Jason from above.

Roy shrugged.

Inside the narrow space between the tiny doors was a small fountain, like the kind Roy had seen on the front lawns of fancy houses, or in front of big hotels.

This fountain was much smaller.

It was almost like a fountain for elves.

"Why would anyone want to steal that?" asked Jason.

Roy shrugged. "And why would anyone keep a running fountain locked up inside the walls?" he said.

< 84 >

"Do you think Uncle Mel put this here?" asked Jason.

"I don't know. But it must have just kept running after he died," Roy said.

"Something's in the water," said Jason. He dipped his hand in the water. "I think it's a piece of wood."

Roy reached in too. "Feels like a fireplace log," he said.

"Very weird," Jason said.

"Hey, what's that?" Roy pointed at something hanging from the other door, on the opposite side of the fountain.

"Give me a boost again," said Jason, and Roy lifted him up.

Jason reached through the door and past the fountain and pulled the thing off the other door.

< 86 >

"A family portrait!" said Roy. They held it together under the light.

Roy had seen old photos like this before. Instead of being in color or even in black and white, they were made of different shades of brown.

The family in the photo was very big, and sitting at the very front was a young boy. Sitting next to the boy was an old man.

Just then, the boys heard a thump from outside the closet.

"Mom must have heard us!" said Roy. "Quick, turn off the light and keep quiet."

Jason hopped up onto Roy's shoulder, pulled on the string, and hopped back down. The brothers huddled in the closet and listened.

They heard more footsteps.

< 87 >

"They're not coming from upstairs," whispered Jason.

"They're coming from the kitchen," said Roy.

Roy listened closely.

The feet making the sounds were slow and heavy. It sounded as if one foot was being dragged across the floor.

< 88 >

# THE LOG

The footsteps moved into the dining room.

Soon the boys heard the scraping of metal on wood coming from the other side of the fountain.

"He's trying to break into that door from the other side," whispered Roy.

Jason shivered and looked at his brother.

"I don't like this, Roy," said Jason. "If he can't get through that door, then he'll come over here to try from this side!"

< 89 >

"Don't worry, Jay," said Roy. "I have an idea!"

The boys listened closely to the scraping. Then it stopped.

And, just as Jason predicted, the footsteps started heading toward the closet.

Roy lifted Jason over the fountain.

Jason unlocked the other door from the inside and swung it open.

Then he climbed out into the dining room.

Roy stepped over the fountain and climbed through the door to follow him.

The dining room was completely dark.

"Jay, where did you go?" Roy whispered into the darkness.

He reached out in front of him to get his bearings and stumbled through the room.

< 90 >

He took a couple of steps and knocked into the table. A statue fell and banged to the ground.

Roy stood very still. He was afraid the noise would alert the intruder. It would let him know that the boys were in the dining room.

Just then, Roy heard someone moving around upstairs, and then a light turned on in the hallway.

A little light shined into the dining room.

Roy heaved a sigh of relief. It must be Mom. She was coming down to see what all the fuss was.

Roy turned around to walk into the hall and then froze.

He was not alone in the dining room.

He was face to face with a walking, breathing skeleton.

< 91 >

Roy turned to run toward the light in the hall, but a cold, bony hand gripped his shoulder.

"Don't," said a voice, dry and dusty. "Don't run!"

Roy spun around. In the dim light he could make out a pair of deep, black eyes and a thin smile. The bald head gleamed like the dull, dusty statues. Freezing fingers dug into Roy's shoulder.

"Leave me alone!" Roy screamed.

"The fountain," said the dry voice of the skeleton. "Did you find the fountain?"

"Fountain?" said Roy. "The one in the wall?" Roy turned to glance at the little door. "Take it! We don't want it!"

"I don't want it either," said the cold voice. "I was just hoping you'd find it."

< 92 >

Without letting go of his grip on Roy, the skeleton reached into the little door.

He grabbed the log from the fountain's pool and pulled it out.

"This is what I came for, Roy Blaze," the skeleton said.

Roy's eyes had gotten used to the dark in the dining room. He could see the skeleton's face more clearly now.

He suddenly realized he was talking to the odd old man from the diner.

"A log?" asked Roy. "What's the big deal about that log?"

"This log," said the old man, "is my life."

He limped over to one of the dining room chairs and sat down.

The effort seemed to have taken all his energy.

< 93 >

Then he motioned for Roy to sit next to him. "Did you see the photo that was hanging here?" the old man asked.

"The old family picture?" said Roy. "Yes. Are you the little boy in it?"

The old man laughed. "In that picture, I am the old man. The little boy is your uncle Mel."

"What? That's impossible," said Roy. "That would mean you're over 150 years old!"

"I turned 450 this spring, to be exact," said the old man.

Roy was speechless.

The old man chuckled, but he quickly became serious again. "That's why I need this log. My mother loved me very much, Roy. I was born here in these woods long before this town was built." He paused and looked around the room.

< 94 >

Then the old man went on, "A shaman from my tribe told her I would not live any longer than this log would burn on our village's fire." The old man held the log tightly against his chest.

"My mother risked her very life to steal this log from the fireside," the old man continued. "She ran from the village, for the shaman did not like her interfering with his prophecy. The men of the village chased her, but she escaped them. And to keep me alive, she watered this log every day until she died."

He went on, "As a young man, and even as an old man, I thought she was foolish. It was a silly story, I said, listening to that foolish shaman. But the log was handed down through my family, and every so often, a believer would be born."

"My uncle Mel?" asked Roy.

< 96 >

The old man nodded.

"So Uncle Mel kept it in this fountain so it could never possibly catch on fire," said Roy, finally understanding.

The old man smiled and said, "He was the last believer. I tried many times to get the log away from him. He was a stubborn man, especially in his old age. But now I finally have it."

"I can take over watering it!" said Roy. "I'm a believer too."

The old man laughed. "You are kind, Roy," he said. There was a long silence.

He placed a bony hand on Roy's shoulder. "I don't need another believer. What I need is a fire in which to throw this log."

"But if you do, you'll die." Roy couldn't believe it.

< 97 >

"Yes," said the old man. "Death will be very welcome. After 450 years of walking this earth, my old bones are tired. Very tired. I just want my rest."

Roy just stood there. For a second he thought about grabbing the log and running away with it to save the old man's life. Why would anyone want to die? he wondered.

A moment later, the lights came on in the dining room, and Mom and Jason were standing in the doorway.

"What is going on?" demanded Mom.

Roy turned around.

The old man was gone.

< 98 >

# CHAPTER 12

# BURNING TREASURE

The next morning, Roy explained the old man's story to his brother.

He wasn't sure Jason really understood it all. He wasn't sure he even understood it himself!

The two boys sat on the porch, drinking their orange juice, and talking about it.

"But what about Larry?" said Jason. "Everything he said on the phone, and getting angry at you. It must have been him!"

< 99 >

Just then, Larry's white pickup drove into the front yard.

A police car followed close behind it.

In less than a minute, the Newcomb brothers were tromping up the front wooden steps. "Where's your mom, boys?" said Larry. "I'm all done with the job."

Roy squinted up at the handyman. "She's in the kitchen," he replied.

The Newcombs walked past the boys.

Then the sheriff said, "Good job, Larry. Now that you finished this job, you can get started with the work out on my place this afternoon."

Roy waited for the front door to close behind the men.

He looked at Jason.

They both laughed.

< 100 >

"That's what Larry was talking about," Roy said. "The sheriff was only asking him to hurry up painting our house so he could go work on his house next. That was his next 'job'!"

"Well, I'm glad we're leaving today," said Jason. "This place gives me the creeps! Even if we have cleaned it all up."

Jason hopped up from his seat and walked into the house.

Roy just sat there, thinking about the weird things that had happened in the last week.

"Hello, Roy," came a voice.

Roy looked up.

He saw a figure standing in the shadow of the woods.

It was the old man.

Roy walked over to him.

< 101 >

"I didn't want to leave without saying goodbye," said the old man. "And I wanted to thank you."

"Sure," said Roy. "You're welcome."

"I guess I should introduce myself," said the man. "My name is Roy Blaze too."

"Really?"

The old man nodded. "It's a longtime family name," he said. "And now finally it's all yours."

He smiled, and this time Roy didn't think his smile was creepy after all.

"Say goodbye to your brother for me, and to your mother. Although she probably doesn't remember me. Just tell her Uncle Roy was here, and that he said goodbye," said the old man.

Roy smiled at his grandfather.

< 102 >

His great-great-great grandfather?

Then Roy watched as the old man walked into the woods, his log under his arm.

* * *

That afternoon, the Blazes's car finally drove away from the strange, giant house.

All their work was done. They'd never see the house again.

As their car headed home, Roy asked, "Mom, did you have an uncle named Roy when you were little?"

Mom thought for a moment. "No," she said, "I didn't."

"Hmm," said Roy.

"But your father did," she added. "A weird, old man. And very old. I only met him once or twice. I don't know what happened to him."

Jason tugged his brother's sleeve.

< 103 >

He pointed out the car's rear window.

Roy turned to look.

Behind the big old house was a blazing orange glow.

It looked like a sunset, but the brothers knew what it really was.

< 104 >

# ABOUT THE AUTHOR

Steve Brezenoff lives in Minneapolis with his wife, Beth, and their small, smelly dog, Harry. Besides writing books, he enjoys playing video games, riding his bicycle, and helping high school students to improve their own writing skills. Steve's ideas almost always come to him in dreams, so he does his best writing in his pajamas.

# GLOSSARY

**ancient** (AYN-shunt)—very old

**billowed** (BIL-ohd)—rose up in large clouds

**demonstrate** (DEM-uhn-strate)—to show people how to do something

**extinguish** (ek-STING-gwish)—to put out

**interfering** (in-tuhr-FEER-ing)—getting in the way, or being involved where you don't belong

**intruder** (in-TROOD-uhr)—someone who is somewhere they don't belong

**Lakota** (la-KOH-tah)—a Native American tribe

**prophecy** (PROF-uh-see)—a prediction

**rubble** (RUHB-uhl)—broken bricks and stones

**shaman** (SHAH-man)—a healer

**skeleton** (SKEL-uh-tuhn)—the bones that make up a body

**tipi** (TEE-pee)—a hut made of poles and covered with bark or animal hides

# DISCUSSION QUESTIONS

1. Why didn't the old man want to live forever?

2. The old man's mother risked her life to steal the log that would keep him alive. Why did she do that?

3. At the diner, Roy saw the old man get a shock from the electric light socket. Why do you think the old man wasn't hurt or killed?

# WRITING PROMPTS

1. Pretend that you have been alive for 450 years. What thing from those years would you most remember? Use a history book to help you write about it!

2. Would you want to live forever if you could? Why or why not?

3. The house that Roy and Jason are staying in is full of strange things. One of the strange things is the small door, where the log was kept. What other things could be behind the door? Write a story about something else the boys could have found there.

# MORE ABOUT . . .

*Burning Secrets* is very loosely based on the ancient Greek tale of Meleager (mel-EE-jer).

When Meleager was born, his mother, Queen Althaea (al-THEE-uh), was visited by the three Fates.

The Fates were powerful women who could predict a person's life. Two of the Fates predicted Meleager would be strong and heroic. The third predicted he would die as soon as a log on the fire burned out completely.

Althaea, because she loved her infant son, pulled the log from the fire and hid it away someplace very safe so that it would never burn completely.

For many years, Meleager was a great hero, and he could not be killed.